Grumpy Cat

to Vincent, Oskar, and Sputnik
Britta Teckentrup

First published in Great Britain in 2008 by Boxer Books Limited.

No part of this publication may be reproduced, stored in a retrieval system, or transmitted in any form or by any means, electronic, mechanical, photocopying, recording, or otherwise, without written permission of the publisher. For information regarding permission, write to Sterling Publishing Co., Inc., 387 Park Avenue South, New York, NY 10016.

ISBN 978-0-545-29320-4

12 11 10 9 8 7 6 5 4 3 2 1   10 11 12 13 14 15/0

Printed in the U.S.A.   08

This edition first printing, September 2010

Grumpy Cat

Britta Teckentrup

SCHOLASTIC INC.
New York Toronto London Auckland
Sydney Mexico City New Delhi Hong Kong

Once there was a cat who lived all alone.

He ate on his own.

He slept on his own.

He spent every day alone.

He would sit between the
trash cans and look very,
very grumpy.

At night, other cats in the neighborhood
would meet and play together.
Cat wanted to join in,
but he just didn't know how.

The other cats didn't ask him because
they thought he was a grumpy cat.
But really—he was a lonely cat.

One night everything changed.
There was a terrible thunderstorm
that crashed and shook the ground.
Cat looked for shelter from the storm,
but there wasn't any.
Poor Cat got wetter, colder, soggier,
and even grumpier than before.

Then suddenly, out of nowhere,
there came a meow. Cat looked
down and there, between his paws,
was a little orange kitten.
Kitten was as wet and as cold
and as soggy as Cat.
"Meow," said Kitten.
Cat didn't know what to do.

The rain stopped.

Kitten meowed again.

She thought she had found a friend.

But Cat just glared at Kitten and walked away.

Kitten followed Cat.

She rolled on her back and showed her belly.

She wiggled her tail
under Cat's nose.

She tried to catch Cat's tail.
She just wanted to be friendly.
But Cat still looked grumpy.

Cat tried his best to lose Kitten
by balancing on a high picket fence.
But Kitten was right behind him.

Cat thought he had finally lost
Kitten by climbing a tall tree.
Then Cat heard a meow.
Slowly and grumpily, Cat turned around.
There at the foot of the tree was Kitten.

Kitten followed Cat up the tree.

She tried to reach him by balancing on the thinnest of branches.

Then Kitten slipped. . . .

Quick as a flash, Cat leaped over
and took Kitten gently by the scruff
of her neck and carried her down
the tree to safety.

Once they were on the ground,
Cat licked Kitten to make sure
she felt safe.

Kitten meowed. She was happy and hungry.

Cat dashed off . . .

but soon returned
with a surprise—
a great, big, fresh fish
as big as Kitten!

Cat and Kitten ate until their bellies were full.

Cat and Kitten cuddled up for a snooze.

They had each found a friend.

And Cat was never grumpy again. . . .

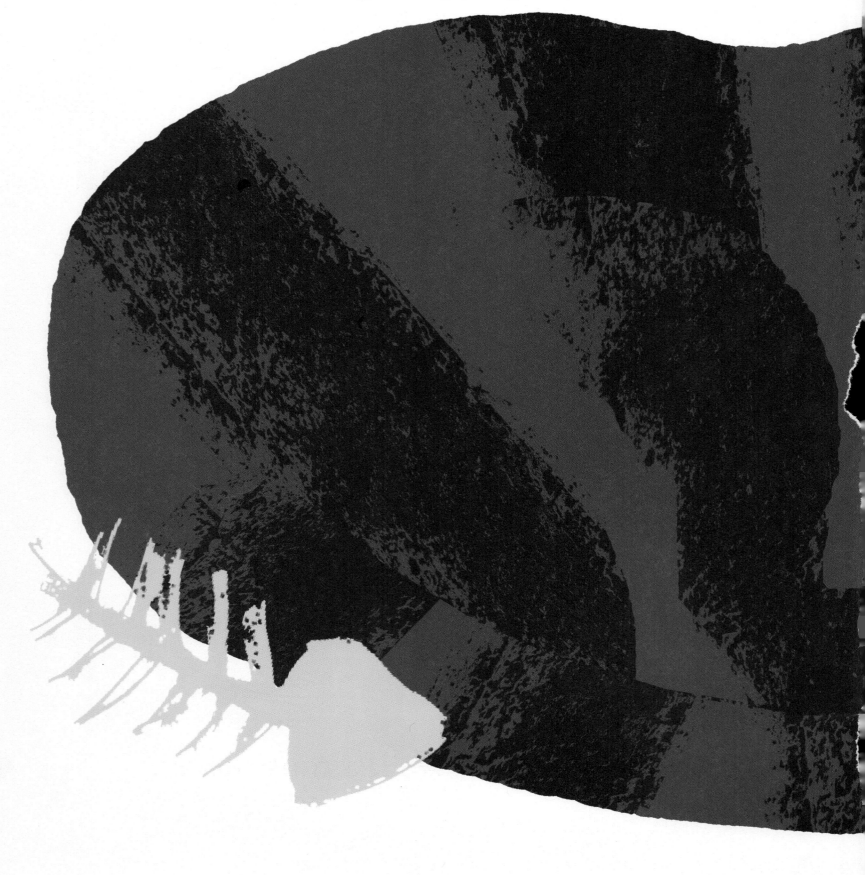

Well, almost never.